Dion Boucicault

Forbidden Fruit

A Comedy in Three Acts

Dion Boucicault

Forbidden Fruit
A Comedy in Three Acts

ISBN/EAN: 9783744783231

Printed in Europe, USA, Canada, Australia, Japan

Cover: Foto ©Andreas Hilbeck / pixelio.de

More available books at **www.hansebooks.com**

FORBIDDEN FRUIT,

A

Comedy in Three Acts,

BY

DION BOUCICAULT, Esq.

FOR PRIVATE USE.—NOT PUBLISHED OR SOLD.

NEW YORK.

1876.

ACT I.

DOVE'S CHAMBERS IN THE TEMPLE.

ACT II.

A RAILWAY STATION.   THE REFRESHMENT ROOM.

ACT III.

THE CREMORNE HOTEL.

ACT I.

SCENE. CATO DOVE'S *Chambers in the Temple. Clerk's Office.* R. H. *Door in partition,* R. C. *Fireplace. Door.* PODD *dis- covered arranging papers,* L. H. *Bell Rings.* PODD *goes into Office,* R. H. *Opens door. Enter* ZULU.

ZULU.—Mr. Cato Dove?

PODD (R. C.)—Will you please to walk in, Ma'am. (*Leads her into Chamber* L. H.) This is his room, (C, *behind table.*) Is it anything I can attend to? I am Mr. Dove's Clerk.

ZULU (R.)—No; I wish to see him personally.

PODD.—He is in the Court at present—we have a motion on the list this morning!

ZULU.—Is it anything interesting on the Brighton Scandal Case?

PODD (*Handing Chair* L.)—No, ma'am. That case stands over till Monday next. May I ask, are you concerned in that matter?

ZULU (*Crossing to* C.)—Oh, very much!

PODD.—A witness, I suppose, ma'am.

ZULU.—Yes, sir; that is what I want to be.

PODD.—For the defense, I presume.

ZULU.—Well, sir, so long as I am a witness, it don't matter to me. (*Sits in Chair* L.)

PODD.—Yes, ma'am; but you see it matters very much to the case. Are you an important witness?

ZULU.—The more important the better—that is what I want to see Mr. Cato about! I want to be well displayed!

PODD.—Well displayed, ma'am! I don't quite understand! (*Bell rings*—R. *up stage in office.*) Oh here is Mr Cato. (*Cross- ing to office.*) I know his pull at the bell—(*Enter office*)—a sort of snatch, as much as to say—It's me and I'm in a hurry! (*Opens door.* PODD *passes into outer office—opens door*). *Enter* MR. CATO DOVE.

CATO.—Any letters? (*Down* R. *to desk, takes off his hat,*

gloves, and gives the " *and his umbrella to* PODD, *who hangs them up at b'ck in office.*)

PODD.—Yes, sir ; three, sir, and a lady.

CATO (*Standing at desk.*)—Oh ! (*pening letters in outer office and reading.*) Um ! um ! um ! What sort of a lady ?

PODD (R. C.)—Very peculiar lady, sir. Some new evidence. —ZULU (*Walks round room—peeps into papers on table*) in the Brighton Scandal case, strange lady, sir—says she wants to be well displayed.

CATO (*Reading and unfoldin; a playbill enc'osed in 2d letter.*)— What's this? Another playbill. Who is this individual who sends me every day her woodcut—(*reads playbill*)—Mdlle. Zulu on the flying trapeze ! Geni of the Ring? (ZULU *who has been examining room, and looking into drawers in table, now mounts on a chair L. H. up stage—to look at a portrait hanging against the wall.*)

ZULU.—I wonder who that is ! She has an ill-tempered mouth whoever she is.

CATO (*Opening another letter reads*)—I forgot to enclose my photogragh. Zulu ! (*Takes Photograph, cabinet size, out of letter.*)

PODD.—Oh, sir—

CATO.—What ?

PODD.—She's in there ! (*Points to Room L H.*)

CATO.—Who ?

PODD.—The photograph, sir ! the lady ! her as wants to be displayed !

CATO,—The original of this likeness—is in my room, waiting for me. Are you sure ?

PODD.—Well, sir, the original in there has got so much dress and so little visible, and this likeness has so little dress and so much visible, that it is hard for me to swear !

CATO (*After crossing to L. of Podd.*)—What can a flying trapeze want with me ? (*After a moment's hesitation—he looks at the photograph and enters the room, finds her perched in the chair.*) What is she about ? I beg your pardon !

ZULU (*Turning on chair.*)—No apology. I was admiring the pluck of that old fellow, to sit tor his portrait at his time of life and in such a wig. What's his line of business?

CATO (*Going to back of the table.*)—That is the Lord Chief Justice !

Zulu (*Leaping down.*)— Thank ye. You don't mind my looking about, I hope?

Cato (*Motioning her t the chair in front. He sits at table.*)—I am sorry to have kept you waiting!

Zulu (*Advancing to L. C.*)—No offence. I suppose you know me, so I need no introduction.

Cato. - I believe I have the pleasure of receiving mademoiselle (*Looking at playbill*) Fooloo?

Zulu. Zulu, sir, not Fooloo. Zulu!

Cato. I beg your pardon. Foreign names are rather confusing.

Zulu. The flying Fairy of the Trapeze—the Geni of the Ring. I see you have received my card.

Cato. I have received your card—yes, that is—I received a——

Zulu. Card de visite.

Cato. Oh, yes--the photograph!

Zulu. You have not seen me at Cremorne?

Cato. I am ashamed to say—that is a pleasure to come.

Zulu. I am the original projectile, sir, the first person that ever submitted to serve as a Cartridge in a Cannon.

Cato (*Rising.*) Bless me my dear lady.

Zulu. Yes, sir, I see the idea takes your breath away. You should see the faces of the public when the cannon is charged, and after leaping lightly on the tip of the muzzle and waving a graceful adieu to a crowd I slide down into the Monster's iron throat! Hurried music in the orchestra—a pause to pile up the agony— Fire, Bang! I am shot in the air to alight like a bird on the rail of a rapeze! The sensation is thrilling, I assure you!

Cato. I feel that effect from your description only. I shall take an early opportunity of being thrilled (*Drawing chair close to her C.*)

Zulu. Much obliged, but to the business that brings me here. Mr. Cato, I have followed the great Brighton Scandal Case in which you are engaged, with the greatest interest. I never miss a day in Court!

Cato. All London is full of it. It is a painful exposure of the inner life of our upper classes.

ZULU. Painful ! Sir, not at all. I am infatuated about it. I cannot get it out of my head I dream of it. I breakfast and dine upon it. I know every one of your speeches by heart.

CATO (*Aside*.) He ! he ! the girl is gone on me. this is a decided case. Ha ! ha ! I am glad my wife is not here !

ZULU. For three years I've worked hard to get well displayed before the public, and never obtained more than three lines in the Daily Press, but here, sir, everybody is talking about the business and witnesses in this case, perfectly unknown people until you called them in the witness-box, once there they get columns of notice—I want to be a witness !

CATO. Dear me, madam, what do you mean ?

ZULU. I want to be in the box, and have you talk to me, and make me tell all my life, I've made out a lovely biography and I want to tell it ! Draw me out as you did that lady you examined yesterday !

CATO But what has your Biography to do with the Brighton Scandal ?

ZULU. No more than the Biography of that lady ; you made her confess a lot of things that had nothing to do with the case, but were so interesting.

CATO. But how can you be connected with it ?

ZULU. Nothing easier, I've thought of that ! You can ask me. (Ah, how well I know the tones of your voice.) " Miss Zulu, you are, I believe, an Equestrian Artiste ?" Yes, sir. 'One of the most distinguished and attractive in your profession ?" Yes, sir. "You remember last Christmas a gentleman sending you some very costly presents of jewelry ?" Really, sir. I receive so many tributes of that description, I cannot, amongst the number, distinguish the particular gentleman to whom you allude ! ' Come, come, Miss Zulu you must know, I mean the defendant in this case ; we are instructed that the defendent fell passionately in love with you last winter, lavished a little fortune on you in diamonds, besieged you with flowers ?" I shall be covered with charming confusion, and you will make the most of it for the amusement of the jury. It will be delightful—you can keep me at it as long as you please !

CATO (*Getting nearer to her.*) It would be more delightful to enjoy your charming confusion here, as long as I pleased.

ZULU. Oh, Mr. Cato—how good you are and how I can scarcely believe my senses that I am really talking to you like this, and there you are ! It is not possible ! It can't be ! I'm afraid it is a dream !

CATO (*His arm over the back of her chair.*) No, it is not a dream —or if it is—don't awake me.

ZULU. Oh, that voice ! how it takes me back into court. What is the emotion that makes my heart throb and takes my breath away, when I am in court is it the depths of interest or the want of ventilation ! (*Cato takes her hand.*) Oh, Mr. Cato don't misjudge me, I am not an ordinary woman.

CATO. Oh, no ! (*Leaning toward her.*)

ZULU. I am a bundle of nerves, an electro-flying machine !

CATO. I am sensible of the fluid !

PODD. Their voices are got very low. I hope Mr. Cato is not getting out of one scandal case into another !

ZULU. Mr. Dove, will you allow me to call you Alfred ? Will you pardon the liberty if I do ? I'll tell you why. I had a friend, a very dear friend. Don't ask me what became of him, but whoever occupies the pedestal of my admiration at which he was the first idol. I call all my idols Alfred !

CATO. I should like to be Alfred the Great ? (*Bell rings.* CATO *rises.*)

ZULU. How provoking !

CATO. (*Aside*) I hope it is not my wife !

(PODD *rises and goes to the door.*)

ZULU. You can see me any evening at Cremorne, or I could come any day here you might be disengaged. How good of you to waste your time on me !

(CATO *listens at door* C.)

PODD *opens the door. Enter* BUSTER.

BUSTER (C.) Dove in ?

PODD (R.) Yes, sir, he is engaged with a client ! (*They speak apart.*)

CATO. It is Mr. Sargeant Buster. (*Returns to* C.)

ZULU We see him nearly every night at Cremorne !

CATO. You shall hear from me,

ZULU. You won't forget me ? (ZULU *goes to Fireplace* L. *and settles her hat in the glass, as they speak.*)

CATO. Impossible !

Zulu. Alfred! (*Points to a portrait on the wall* L.) Who is that person?

Cato (*Aside,*) My wife. (*Aloud.*) That, oh, that is, a—Mrs. Buster. You see Buster occupies these chambers jointly with me!

Zulu. Oh, that's Mrs. Buster; I'm sorry for Buster, she is a cat. (*Enter* Buster *into* L. H. *room.* Zulu *pulls down her veil.*) Good day. I hope I have not intruded on too much of your time (*Going out*)

(Buster *retires up* C.)

Cato. Not at all! (*Following her to the door*) Good day!

Zulu. Good day. (*She bows to* Buster, *then says as she goes out. aside.*) I am sorry for Buster. (*Crosses office. Podd opens door for her;* Zulu *exits* Buster *crosses to fireplace.* Cato *after seeing her out returns to* L. H. *room and shuts the door.* Buster *stands with back to fire, turning faces* Cato.)

Buster, (*Looks at* Cato *significantly.*) If you have another client or two of that kind, I'll exchange with you a good—er—a railway case against one of them.

Cato, (*Crossing to table* C. *sits as he speaks.*) My dear Buster, you are a dissipated luminary of the law. Your head is always running on petticoats. (*Sits at table and begins fussing amongst his papers*) I assure you that was a—a perfect lady, but I know your disrespect for the sex leads you to form ideas!

Buster. Cato, thou reasonest well! What are you looking for? (*Advances to* L. *of table.*)

Cato. The Vice-Chancellor's opinion *in re* Tollemache.

Buster, (*Picks up Zulu's photo.*) Is this it? (*Hands him it.*)

Cato. Zulu!

Buster. Oh, it was Zulu? I thought I recognized her chin, and that equestrian swing in her walk—she cannot get—er—a—the trapeze out of it. My dear Cato, I congratulate you!

Cato. Now, Buster, really I don't like this kind of joke; it is in your way, I know—you go in for this sort of thing, but please to recollect I am a married man!

Buster. So am I, very much married. I—er—a don't know a man more married than I am! (*Crosses to* R)

Cato. I love my wife!

Buster. So do I; that is, when I say your wife, I mean my wife!

CATO, (*Rising and going to fireplaces*). Yes, sir, everybody's wife—anybody's wife that will give you the slightest encouragement.

BUSTER Cato, don't be a fraud; pull down your flag! How would you like this specimen of a client to be submitted to the scrutiny of Mrs. Cato Dove?

CATO Josephine?

BUSTER. Yes, Josephine; the unhappy Josephine; you designing Napoleon!

CATO. My dear Buster. (*Meets him* C.)

BUSTER (R.) Confess, then, or I shall produce this evidence in court! (CATO *tries to snatch the photo from him*) Pull down your flag!

CATO (L.) I—I——; yes, but I assure you this interview was not my seeking! (*Goes up stage to table, followed by* BUSTER.) I never saw her before in my life; never heard of her. I—I found her here, and—— (*Down R.*)

BUSTER, (*Following him.*) Don't be mean Cato; don't he a coward as well as a fraud I have seen her sitting in court every day.

CATO. You have eyes everywhere.

BUSTER. Yes, wherever there is a pretty woman! I marked her down thought—er—a I had scored one, my wish was father to that thought; 'twas you who were the object of her attention, not the deponent. Well?

(*During this scene* PODD *is seated at desk looking over playbill.*)

CATO. She wants to be a witness in the Brighton scandal case! (*Poking fire.*)

BUSTER, (*Looking at photo.*) I'll go down to Cremorne to-night and serve a subpœna upon her myself!

CATO. Don't be a fool!

BUSTER. It is the only character in which to approach a woman, effectually—it—er—a—reconciles her to the superiority of our sex.

CATO. There is no resisting you!

BUSTER. I wish you could make the women think so my dear fellow! But in the mean time it gives me the greatest pleasure to welcome you as a fellow sinner. Your fidelity to Mrs. D. radiated a kind of cold atmosphere of propriety around you that chilled my good fellowship!

Cato. Mephistophiles!

uster. So, to inaugurate the occasion, let us make a night of it; be a bachelor for twenty-four hours! You have had too much cannubulating lately, a little change of air will do you good!

Cato. But my wife?

Buster. It will do her good; you are running down dear boy; you want tone. Your mind is getting contracted within the limits—er—a—of your hearthrug, where you are becoming a mere—er a—domestic machine, of which your wife is the motive power!

Podd (*in the office*).—If that woman comes slinging her trapeze here Mrs. Cato will give her an engagement.

Cato (*bringing Buster down*).—That is perfectly true! Buster, do you know she is growing terribly jealous

Buster.—Do you know why?

Cato.—No.

Buster.—You have never given her any cause!

Cato.—I can't follow your reasoning.

Buster.—There is no reason in a woman's caprices. She is jealous because—er—a—she has nothing else to do!

Cato.—It is very ungrateful of her to suspect me, for I have not deserved it.

Buster (R.)—That's wrong. Deserve it—justify her suspicion and spare her your reproaches by taking her sin on your shoulders. The fact is, she finds you so perfect that she is impatient to discover a fault in you; be generous—gratify her!

Podd (*Still looking over the play-bill*)—She wants to be well displayed. Well, if Mrs. Cato, his wife, catches her, she'll get all the display she wants.

Cato (L.)—I dare not look at a woman in the streets, but my wife asks me what I see in her to stare at? If I draw a deeper breath than usual, she wants to know what I am sighing about? If I put on a decent cravat when I go out, she inquires who I am dressing myself up to captivate? I am afraid to have eyes, lungs, clothes. (*Crosses to* R.)

Buster.—All your fault! Look at my Arabella. Distrust is—er—a firmly established in her mind, and she is thus relieved from all anxiety. Put yourself under my treatment. I am an old practitioner. I shall send Arabella a note not to expect me home to dinner, as I have a consultation at er – a—let me see - at Not-

tingham, this evening. which may detain me until to-morrow morning. So I shall tell her not to wait up for me in case I am detained !

CATO.—Does she stand that ?

BUSTER.—Broke her in early. You must give the same excuse to your wife.

CATO —I could not tell Josephine a lie if I tried. I should stammer, color up to the roots of my hair. I know I should.

BUSTER.—Then write her a note. Notes don't stammer Ink don't blush.

CATO.—I am half inclined, only to give Josephine a lesson.

BUSTER (*Sitting down* R. *of table and writing*)—There is a charming lady engaged in the same troupe with Zulu, Madame Closerie Dililah. I am writing to her to join our party. You write to Zulu. We can secure a private supper room overlooking the gardens—supper for four—it will be delightful !

CATO.—Egad ! I've a good mind.

BUSTER.—Then don't change it. (*Finishes letter.*) That's done. She'll come.

CATO (*Sits to* L *of table. About to write*)—What shall I say ?

BUSTER (*Dictating*)—To-night, after the performance, happy to see you at supper, in reference to your desire to appear as a witness.

CATO (*writing*).—At supper !

BUSTER. Don't sign your name ; I never do. You ought to have an alias to sign it.

CATO. I have one (*signing*)—Alfred.

BUSTER (*goes to door, calls*)—Podd !

PODD. Sir ? (*Rises and crosses to door.*)

BUSTER. Post these letters immediately. (*Hands letters to him*).

PODD. Very good, sir.

BUSTER. No, wait a moment ; there are two other letters you may take at the same time.

PODD. Shall I copy these into the letter-book, sir ? (*Going back to desk* R.)

BUSTER, No ! (*Shuts the door.*) What an old fool. (*Returns to table.*) Now then sit down there and write to your wife, and I will write to mine.

CATO. Oh, lord ! what shall I say ?

BUSTER Follow my style. Affectionate, but off hand. Are you ready?

CATO. All right. My hand trembles so.

PODD (*Reading addresses*)—Madame Closerie Dalilah, Mademoiselle Zulu, Robinson's Circus, Cremorne Gardens. (*Holding letter in one hand and in the other the play-bill.*) I'm not surprised at uster. He always was a music hall Don Juan. He married his houskeeper, a decent woman, who made his home so respectable he can't bear to live in it. But to think Mr. Cato should leave a pretty, lady-like, devoted wife for such an article as this.

(CATO *sits* R *of table.*)

BUSTER. You must write to the same effect that I do. (*writing*). My angel—

CATO (*writing*). My darling—

BUSTER. This infernal Brighton scandal case—

CATO. This eternal Brighton scandal case—

BUSTER. Obliges me to run down this evening to Nottingham—

CATO. Calls me away to Nottingham this afternoon—

BUSTER. To attend a consultation.

CATO. To see a witness.

BUSTER So do not wait up for me to-night after twelve.

CATO. I may be detained very late—so you need not sit up.

BUSTER. It is an infernal nuisance, old Girl.

CATO. This is an awful bore, Ducky.

BUSTER. Go to bed early.

CATO. I shan't go to bed at all.

BUSTER. Your own Charley --

CATO.—Your devoted Catydid.

(*They fold—enclose and direct the Letters.*)

BUSTER.—There. Podd can take this letter to a commissionaire, who will deliver them about the hour we are supposed to be getting on board the train—(*calls*) Podd – (*Rings a gong bell on the table.*)

PODD (*Rises.*)—Yes, sir. (*Enters room.*) (CATO *goes to fireplace—leans on Mantel.*)

BUSTER.—Take these letters to a Messenger and tell him to deliver them; there's the money! (*Hands him a piece of Silver.*)

PODD.—Very good, sir! (*Returns to inner Room.*)

BUSTER.—Well, Cato, how do you feel?

CATO. I don't know whether I feel frightened or happy, it is quite a novel sensation—it is like being in the Dock!

PODD (*reading addresses*)—Mrs. Cato Dove—Mrs. Charles Buster! (*Cato walks about—Buster follows him.*)

CATO.—A day of freedom—a whole Holiday!

BUSTER.—Rule Britannia! Britons never shall be slaves. Where shall we dine?

CATO.—I don't think I could eat a morsel just now! My heart is up here, in my throat. (*Returns to Mantlepiece, L.*) I must digest that before I could swallow anything—Buster!

BUSTER (R.)—What?

CATO.—I am beginning to funk fearfully—what shall I say, how shall I look, when I return home? Josephine will want me to give her chapter and verse for everything—I know her, she will expect a full account of all the consultation!

BUSTER.—Give her a page out of—a—a Chitty on Contracts; she will never stand it to the end—a—a—I never could!

CATO.—Buster! (*faintly*) where do you keep your Brandy?

BUSTER (*goes up to the back C.*) Here it is; what's the matter? Fright?

CATO—Yes, I think it is going for my stomach!

(*Buster brings from a tin box, marked " Private Accounts,' two case flasks.*)

PODD (*In the office, having taken his hat and umbrella.*)—Now to find the Messenger! (*As he opens the door—Mrs. Cato Dove and Mrs. Buster appear at it—coming in*)—Mrs. Cato!

JOSEPHINE (*Entering the Clerk's Office.*)—Yes, I met Mrs Buster in Regent street, and we thought we might drop in and give our husbands a surprise!

(*Enter MRS. BUSTER.*)

ARABELLA (C.) I suppose they are still in Court?

JOSEPHINE (R. C.)—No, Cato told me he would be home early to day!

PODD (R.)—These letters are for you, Ladies. I was just taking them to a Messenger. (*Hands letters to the Ladies.*)

(JOSEPHINE *takes letter and crosses to* L.)

JOSEPHINE.—A letter for me? (*opening it.*)

ARABELLA (*Takes letter down* R.)—Some excuse, I suppose, to dine out, as usual! (*opening hers.*)

JOSEPHINE (*Reading.*)—Oh, dear! what is this? Going out of Town?

ARABELLA.—Nottingham! that means out all night!

PODD (C.)—The gentlemen have not started yet—they are in there. at work.

BUSTER (*To Cato.*)—Take it straight—

JOSEPHINE.—Are they very busy?

(*The two men drink out of the flask.*)

PODD.—They have a case in hand, I believe!

BUSTER.—D'ye feel better? .

CATO.—I think I've got it under!

(*Buster goes behind table C.*)

ARABELLA.—Shall we interrupt them?

JOSEPHINE.—Dear old Catydid—he works too hard! I'll ask him to take me down to Nottingham with him!

(*They enter the R. H. Room.*)

CATO.—Josey!

BUSTER.—My Wife!

(*They hide the flasks in their Coat pockets.*)

JOSEPHINE—How pale he is! (*crosses to L.*) My dear. really you are overdoing it. Isn't he overdoing it, Mr. Buster?

BUSTER.—That is—er—a—just what I have been talking to him about—he should give himself a Holiday!

JOSEPHINE—What is this dreadful news? You are obliged to go to Nottingham?

(ARABELLA *goes up*—BUSTER *down* R.)

BUSTER (R.)—You see how it affects him! Ever since I told him that he must go—he has been like that!

PODD.—Now to post this letter to Mrs. Dalilah! (*Puts on his hat, takes his umbrella and goes out.*)

(ARABELLA (C. *back of Table.*)—I smell Brandy, strongly—

BUSTER.—Brandy impossible! (*aside*) I forgot to cork it, and it is overflowing in my pocket! (*aloud*) Oh, true, I forgot; Dove felt queer and took a nip!

JOSEPHINE.—Darling! I cannot let him go alone!

CATO.—Josey, I must do my duty—but duty must be done without flinching! (*crosses to L. C.*)

BUSTER.—England expects that every man this day shall do his duty!

JOSEPHINE.—Can't I go and do it with you, dear?

CATO.—No, we start immediately. Buster, when do we start?

BUSTER.—By the five o'clock Express—we may be detained all night!

JOSEPHINE AND ARABELLA —All night?

(*Arabella down* C.)

BUSTER (R. C)—There is no knowing what circumstances may arise. We are going to attend the bedside of an invalid witness in our great case?

JOEPHINE.—That horrid Scandal!

BUSTER.—Her evidence is vital!

JOSEPHINE.—Her! Is it a she? (*Crosses to* C.)

BUSTER.—An aged lady of ninety-two.

JOSEPHINE.—Oh! (*relieved*) ninety-two!

BUSTER.—Last birthday!

ARABELLA (*aside*)—Buster is lying! There is an assumption of stupidity about his mout , that he always prepares. when it frames a lie.

JOSEPHINE.—But can't I go with you, dear? Do let me, you won't find me in the way a bit!

CATO (L. *aside*)—Oh, Lord, wouldn't I? (*aloud*) My precious, do be reasonable, bear up, don't add to my difficulties—how could you leave time without a—a—a——

BUSTER.—A toothbrush—er—a—frisette, or—a— a razor?

JOSEPHINE.—I can drive home and pack my traveling bag!

BUSTER.—We have not more than forty minutes to catch the Express.

JOSEPHINE (*Stamping with childish grief*) Oh! oh! what shall I do all this evening alone?

CATO.—My angel! (*They speak aside at fireplace.*)

ARABELLA (*who has been watching Buster*)—Charley, dear——

BUSTER —What does my Bonanza want?

ARABELLA (*Taking him aside*)—One lawyer is quite enough to get the evidence of this old party at Nottingham. Cato Dove will go down alone—he is your Junior Counsel; it is *his* business to get up the case.

BUSTER.—My beauty, I—er —shall be wanted!

ARABELLA.—Yes, *I* want you at home to-night, and home you must be, that is if you wish me to sign these papers. (*Produces deed.*)

BUSTER.—What's that?

ARABELLA.—The conveyance of the land you are selling at Paddington.

BUSTER.—Oh, true, has—er—a the attorney sent the deed?

ARABELLA.—Yes, here it is, he came with it to me this morning to obtain my signature.

BUSTER.—Oh ! a mere matter of form.

ARABELLA.—Precisely—but without that mere form, you can't sell the land and get the money, can you ?

BUSTER. —Er—a well a ——

ARABELLA,—You can't. I know it—now if you dine at home like a good boy, and take me to the opera afterwards, I will sign the paper before I go to bed to-night !

BUSTER —What insect have you got down your back, my darling ?

ARABELLA.—No matter about the insect, you know my terms. (*Goes up* R., *crosses over to* L. *behind table.*)

BUSTER (*aside with conviction*)—She is a very superior woman.

JOSEPHINE.—Will you promise to send me a telegram from Nottingham the moment you arrive there ?

CATO. – But my angel, I shall be back so soon.

JOSEPHINE.—No matter I want to be sure you are thinking of me, and not of anyone else.

CATO.—Oh ! oh! as if I could—you will get the message by— let me see—Buster, when can Josey get my message from Nottingham ?

BUSTER.—From Nottingham? Arrive Nottingham 8 o'clock, and give two hours—say two hours—for transmission and de- livery—well, about 10.

JOSEPHINE.—I shall put it under my pillow and cry myself asleep over it ! (*She embraces him and cries.*)

(BUSTER *goes up* R.)

CATO (*speaking over her shoulder*)—Oh ! (*aside*)—'Pon my life, it is too bad, I can't stand this much longer !

BUSTER (R.)—There, Mrs. B., look at that picture of connubial confidence ! Why don't we assume occasionally that attitude.

ARABELLA. (C.)—Because we should laugh over each others shoulders, Mr. B.

BUSTER (*aside, coming down* R.)—She is a very superior woman.

(CATO *goes up to table*).

JOSEPHINE.—Since you must let me see the last of you, I can go with you to the station, can't I ? Do let me ?

CATO (*making up papers in a roll.*)—Certainly, my dear, of course, it will be very much out of your way—we must take a Hansom cab, and I—I don't like you to be seen in Hansom cabs—it looks so fast—Don't it look fast, Buster?

BUSTER.—Very bad form, indeed. (*Crosses to fireplace*).

CATO (R. *of table*)—Even coupes are going out, aint they, Buster?

BUSTER (*at fireplace*) They are called loose boxes!

JOSEPHINE (L. *of table*)—They may call them what they like. I am going to the station with you in your Hansom cab, in defiance of all the proprieties! When you took me to Mabille in Paris on our wedding trip, I was timid—but you overruled my objection by saying: "If a married woman can't defy proprieties under the protection of her husband, what's the advantage of the bonds of wedlock, she obtains her freedom from prejudices by giving up her liber y." I got your very words by heart!

CATO.—My love, of course I shall be delighted—(*aside*). What the devil shall I do now? (*Aloud*)—How are you going Buster?

ARABELLA (R.)—Mr. Buster is going with me!

BUSTER (*aside.*)—Taken in charge.

ARABELLA.—Mr. Podd.

PODD (*at door.*)—Yes, ma'am!

ARABELLA ——Please call up two Hansom Cabs! (*goes up.*)

BUSTER (*crosses to door.*) —Two cabs, Podd---pick out clean ones (*Leaning out of door.*)—Hist, Podd!

PODD.—Sir!

BUSTER (*whispers.*)—Don't post that letter to Cremorne!

PODD.—It is gone, sir!

BUSTER.—Oh, Lord!

PODD (*going out.*)—I see, Mrs. Buster has served a writ of *ne exeat* on the sergeant!

The two ladies look into mirror over mantel-piece. CATO *joins* BUSTER R.)

CATO (R. C. *aside to Buster.*)—Buster—here's a go!

BUSTER (R.)—Yes, it is a go to Nottingham!

CATO.—What on earth shall we do there?

BUSTER.—Arabella has cornered me—I can't accompany you.

CATO.—What? Oh, I say—I'm not going to be expressed to Nottingham! What's to be done? You got me into this scrape.

BUSTER.—I like that—didn't I find you in it? Over head and ars in it—with Zulu?

Cato. —I can't go wandering about the Midland Counties all night. What's to be done ? I feel like a drowning man !

Re-enter Podd *into office.*

Buster. —Then don't struggle—lie on your back and think—stop! could not you get rid of her at the station, and slip out, leaving the train to start without you ?

Cato. —Splendid—I'll do it !

Podd (*looking in.*)—The cabs are at the door, sir !   *(He retires.*

Josephine. —Now, darling, I am ready.

Arabella. —Now, Charley, give me your arm !

Josephine. —Poor Caty, he *does* look sorry to go ! Well, that is some comfort, I never saw him look so vexed. Don't dear. There, I won't leave you till I see the train off !

Cato (*aside.*)—Oh, Lord !   (*He looks desparingly at Buster.*)

Josephine. —You shall see the very last glimpse of me !

Cato (*aside*)—I am in for it.   There is no escape ! What a night I shall pass !

Arabella.—Now ; Sergeant, I am yours until to-morrow !

Buster (*aside*)—Oh, Lord ! What a night we both shall pass !

THE ACT DROP FALLS

AS THEY GO OUT.

ACT II.

SCENE—*The refreshment saloon of a railway station. Large glass doors at back* L. H. *looking out on the street. " Ladies' Waiting Room"* R. H. *Refreshment counter* R. H. *at back. Door* L. H. 2d E. *Entrance to railway platform. Girl discovered behind counter* R. *Enter* CAPT. DERRINGER *and a railway* PORTER *carrying his valise* L. H. D.

DERRINGER (R. C.)—Leave my valise there, and call me a cab.

PORTER (*Places valise up* L.)—A Hansom, sir, or a 4-wheeler?

DER. (*Crosses to* R.)—How delightful is that familiar sound ! A Hansom cab ! It is four years since I rode in one. (*Back to* C.) No, my friend—get me a 4-wheeler. as I have my luggage here—it will be more convenient.

POR.—All right, sir. (*Exit D. in* F. *and off* R.)

DER. (*Crosses to* L.)—Home again, after four years in India. How green the fields looked as we swept along—how cheerful every face appeared !

(*Railway* PORTER *outside heard to whistle and cry*) :

POR —Four-wheeler !

DER.—Nothing changed since I left this very railway station in '72. I think I can recollect that very girl behind the counter ; they have not changed her. Dear old England ! with all my faults, I love thee still ! (*Takes out a cigar.*) Yes, nothing changed—(*Up* C. *to counter*)—I recognize those cakes under a gla s case—they are the very same ! (*To the* GIRL.) My dear, can you give me a glass of ale ?

GIRL.—Yes, sir, if you please.

DER.—Can you oblige me with a match to light my cigar?

GIRL.—No matches, sir. Smoking is not allowed in this room —it is against the company's rules.

DER —Of course ; dear old prejudices—fine old crusted conservative habits. (*Feels in his p cket.*) If I had a piece of paper I might get a light at this lamp. (*Takes out a letter, rolls it up.*) I never knew an English rule could not be covered with half a crown. (*Lights the paper at a lamp* R.)

GIRL (R. C. *serving him*).—Glass of hale, sir—three pence—Hallsopp !

DER.—Glass of hale—Hallsopp's hale ; there's ten shillings—pray keep the change—and the H's.

GIRL.—Hoh, sir !

DER.—Her sweet cockney voice is worth the money ! (*He throws down the letter half consumed, and treads upon it—taking up glass.*) My dear, here's a good husband to you ! (*Drinks.*)

GIRL.—I've got an 'usband, sir.

DER.—Then here's a second one with an H, for a change. (*Drinks.*) By Jove ! (*Crosses to L.*) what a surprise my arrival will be to my sister, Josephine. I hope I shall not find her changed after so long an absence, but marriage does make such a difference in women ; it makes none in men ; that's natural, of course. I wonder what sort of a fellow her husband is—(*crosses up to C. to finish ale.*)—Dove,—what a name for a chap—and for a lawyer, too. I think she says in her letter he is a lawyer or a doctor—I forget which. (*Drinks.*) Well, I never thought Josey would have thrown herself away on a lawyer—(*down R.*)—when she might have had her pick of the army list ; now if she had married a sawbones, he might have joined a regiment !

(*Re-enter railway* PORTER, D. *in* F.)

POR. (*up L.*)—Here is your 4-wheeler, sir. (*Picks up the valise.*) Where shall I tell the driver to take you, sir ?

DER (R.)—Oh, true, my sister's address ; I forget the number—it is in her letter—(*feels in his pocket*)—at the top of her letter—the only one I have received from her these twelve months. Where have I put it ?—(*crosses to L. C.*)—it was certainly in this pocket. Oh. the deuce ! (*Turns up.*) I can't have lighted my baccy with it, surely ? (*Picks up the half consumed letter.*) I have though, here it is ! (*Reads.*) "Your affectionate sister, Josey " — but the address is burned off ! What's to be done now ? Oh, stay ! (*Turns to the* GIRL.) Will you oblige me with a look at your directory ?

GIRL (C.)—We don't keep one, sir.

POR. (L.)—You will find one at the newspaper shop, there's one in the next street—I'll show the driver where it is.

DER. (R.) That's a good fellow. Dove ! There cannot be many doves in London ! I shall look down the list of Doves

in the directory, and easily pick out my brother. I hope the human Dove does not take after the prolific bird (*going up*), or I shall be hunting Doves all day long.

POR. (*going up.*) – This way, sir.

As they go up, enter ZULU D. *in* F. *from* R.

ZULU (*down* R.)—How provoking! I've just missed the 4.40 train

DER. (L. C.)—By Jove—what a splendid girl !

ZULU (*To* DER)—Can you tell me, sir, if the five o'clock down train stops at Barnet? I want to go to Barnet.

DER.—Would you accept a share of my cab?

ZULU.—Sir ! what do you take me for? But perhaps 'tis I who am mistaken. Are you not a railway official ?

DER (L)—Unfortunately, no. I wish I was. I am only a lieutenant of artillery.

ZULU (R.)—Oh, sir, a thousand pardons—you have a sort of uniform look that deceived me !

DER.—Don't mention it. Can I be of service ?

ZULU.—I have a letter for a lady who resides at Barnet—Madame Closerie Dalilah—it is an invitation to supper to-night, at Cremorne, and it must be delivered to her in time.

DER.—Cremorne, Dalilah—surely her name is familiar to me.

ZULU.—Mine is not unknown to fame, sir—I am the great Zulu ! (*The* PORTER *drops the valise.*) The Geni of the Ring. I may say, sir, that I'm in the artillery, also—for we have a real gunner in his full uniform to fire me off every night.

DER. (*bowing.*)—I wish I was the target.

ZULU.—I trust to rank you amongst my supporters ; but how shall I get this letter to Closerie?

POR.—Why don't you telegraph?

ZULU.—I never thought of that !

POR.—There's an office inside on the platform—it's only a shilling message.

ZULU (*Crosses to* R. H.)—I could have done that at Chelsea. How thoughtless I was to come all this way when I might have spared myself the trouble and the cab fare.

DER. (R.)—Allow me to bless your thoughtlessness, as it bestows on me the pleasure of your acquaintance.

ZULU.—Oh, sir. (*Aside.*) What a nice man !

DER. (*bowing*)—Hoping we shall meet again, allow me to offer you my card.

ZULU.—Here is mine. Always at home, in the ring, from nine to ten P. M.

DER.—True, I forgot! (*Hands her a card.*)

ZULU.—Reserved seats, half a crown! (*Hands him a play-bill Courtesies and exits* L. DERRINGER *opens bill and goes out reading;* C. PORTER *goes with him leaving the valise.*)

GIRL —Well. the imperance of that woman! to go and make the acquaintance of such a splendid young man off-hand like that! What he could see in her. (*Railway Porter returns*). Did you see that. Jim?

PORTER —What—See her fired off at Cremorne Circus? Yes, and there's no fraud about it neither—real powder—the public feels of it afore it goes into the big gun—a real soldier to touch it off. She's a regular good plucked 'un, I tell you!

GIRL.—Good plucked! I should think she was? See her fire herself off at the gentleman?

(*Enter* MR. *and* MRS. CATO DOVE, *and* MR. *and* MRS. BUSTER.)

JOSEPHINE (R.)—Ten minutes to five. I wish we had been too late!

BUSTER (C.)—Now, ladies, you had better sit down in the waiting-room, while Cato and I get the tickets!

JOS.—I'll go with him.

BUSTER —By no means. I'll go. He can stay with you!

JOS.—My dear Sergeant, how good you are.

CATO (R. C.)—What is the fare? No matter; there's a five pound note!

BUSTER (*Aside to* CATO).—It is all right. I have thought of a rescue—leave it to me. (*Exit* L. H. *door*).

ARAB. (L., *looking after him.*)—My mind is not that easy it ought to be; Buster does not inspire me with confidence.

CATO (*Aside, crossing to* R)—A rescue! What does he mean? (*Aloud.*) This way. my dear! (*Going to waiting-room.*)

GIRL.—Beg pardon. sir. no gentlemen are admitted there! That's the rules of the company.

JOS. (R C.)—What a shame!

GIRL.—There's a gentleman's waiting-room, second door on the right.

JOS.—That will do! (*Going* L *with* CATO *and* ARABELLA.)

GIRL.—Beg pardon. ma'am, no ladies are admitted there!

ARAB.—The sexes are committed to solitary confinement.

CATO.—That's the rule of the company. (*Enter Conductor of the Train, who goes to refreshment bar and drinks.*) My dear, you can't stop here in a drinking saloon; wait inside a moment until Buster returns.

JOSEPHINE *and* ARABELLA *enter room* R. H. *Re-enter* BUSTER.

BUSTER (L.)—Here's the tickets. (*Gives him a railway ticket.*)

CATO (R.)—What's this? Why this is a ticket to Hornsey.

BUSTER.—Hush! Don't you see, your wife will see you off by the Nottingham Express I find the train will stop at Hornsey, two miles off you jump out; return here and meet me at Cremorne.

CATO —But she will expect to receive a telegram from me to-night from Nottingham.

BUSTER —I've fixed that all right (*Calls*) Conductor!

CONDUCTOR (C.)—Yes, sir. (*Touches his cap and advancing*)

BUSTER.— You go with the five o'clock Express to Nottingham?

CON.—Yes, sir.

BUSTER.—Could you send a telegram for this gentleman when you arrive there, and accept this sovereign for the trouble? (*Gives him money.*)

CON.—Certainly, sir, there is a telegraph office at the Nottingham station. Where is the message?

BUSTER (*Cross to C. To* CATO).—Go and write it—quick, you have not a minute to lose. Don't stand there like an idiot.

CATO (*Crosses to C.*)—I feel like one; all this is so complicated.

CON (L.)—This way, sir.

CATO (*Going* L.)—I'm so confused. I don't know what to say

BUSTER (*Following him to* L.)—Make it hot and strong, with a squeeze of despair!

Exit CATO, L. H. D. *with* CONDUCTOR

BUSTER (*Returning to* C.)—I would write it for him, but my style is too high flavored. Now, Cato, will come back and we can have a glorious carouse. I have extricated him splendidly! That move is Napoleonic, and he does not appreciate it! Yet nothing is more simple. After a painful parting, I tear the two ladies away and carry them home, and in ten minutes Cato will return here, while the telegram is speeding to Nottingham. from whence it will be dispatched to-night, affording legal evidence of his presence a hundred miles from London, while he will be enjoying a rosy time! Oh, stolen hours are sweet!

(*Re-enter* JOSEPHINE R. H. *door*).

Jos. (R.)—Where's my husband ?

Bus. (C.)—Gone to buy the evening paper—(*Re-enter* ARABELLA R. H. *door*)—and a work of fiction !

(*Re-enter* ZULU L. H. *door*).

ZULU.—That is done. I hope Closerie will come ; I am sure she will !

Bus. (*Aside*).—ZULU, by all the artillery.

ARAB. (R.)—(*measuring* ZULU).—What a very loud person ! Josephine, my dear, Cato was right—this is not a proper place for us ! (*Crosses to* R. C) Serjeant, give me your arm ! (*Up* L.)

Jos. (R. *aside*).—How the creature stares at me ! I hope she is not going by the same train as Cato.

ZULU.—Why, surely, 'tis Mr. Buster !

(*Re-enter* CATO L. H. *door*).

CATO (*crosses to* R. C.)—I have secured a corner seat.

Jos.—I hope you are going in the smoking carriage.

CATO.—My dear, I don't smoke.

Jos. (R. C.)—No matter ! I insist on your going in the smoking carriage !—(*Aside*).—There are no ladies admitted there !—rules of the company.

CATO (C. *aside*).—Zulu, the devil !

ZULU (*aside*).—Alfred !

(PORTER *appearing at* L. H. *door*).

POR.—Now, sir ; if you are going to Nottingham you have no time to lose.—(*Business*).

ZULU (*aside crosses to* R.)—Going to Nottingham ! but how about our supper to-night?

CATO.—Come, Josey, don't you hear ? Oh, Lord ! (*Bell heard outside*).

POR. (*shouting at door* L. H.)—Passengers for Bedford, Nottingham, Leeds and the north. (*Disappears*).

(*Exit* JOSEPHINE *and* CATO L. H. *door*).

ARAB.—Serjeant, that person knows you and Cato ! Who is she ?

Bus.—My dear, she is—er—a—simply—a—a witness in our scandal case!

Arab.—Yes, sir; I should say she has been witness of a good many. (*Look at her with her glasses.*)

Zulu (*to the* Girl *at the bar*).—One of the penalties public people have to endure, is being stared at by the crowd.

Arab. (*aside*).—Impudent baggage! (*Aloud*).—Come, Serjeant! (*Exit* L. H. *door*).

Bus. (*hastily*).—Have you received the letter?

Zulu.—Of course, I have; and have invited my friend to supper!

Bus —All right; we shall be there!

(*Re-enter* Arabella L. H. *door*).

Arab.—Sergeant!

Bus.—My dear! (*Exit with her* L. H. *door*).

Zulu.—She has got the whip hand of him. Well, to see that man in court—brow-beating the judges, bullying the witnesses, and laying down the law to the jury, and then see him here cowed by a petticoat—one would never think it was the same person. (*Mimicking*). Serjeant, my dear! (*Exit* L. H. *door*).

(*Re-enter* Derringer (C.) *with a paper in his hand*).

Der. (R. C.)—I found half a column of Doves in the directory —here they are—27 of them beginning with Aaron and ending with William Dove. I forget my Dove's name. I thought it was a Cæsar or Brutus. Where the deuce shall I begin?

(*Re-enter* Josephine L. H. *door*).

Jos. (L.)—He has gone, dear old boy—he recovered his spirits just at the last!

Der. (R.)—I must take a cab by the hour and call on every Mrs. Dove on the list!

Jos.—Dove, who's this? Why, oh, I cannot be!

Der.—I'll knock one over after the other! Let me see!

Jos.—It is—it is!

Der.—I will begin with Mrs. Dove, 24 Bedford Square.

Jos.—No, begin with Mrs. Dove, 62 Boston Road.

Der.—Sure, it isn't!

Jos.—Yes, it is!

Der.—Joscy !

Jos.—My dear Jack ! (*They embrace*).

Der.—Lord, what luck ! why, do you know, I burned your letter by mistake, and forgetting your address, I was preparing to look up every Dove in London.

Jos.—But why did you not write to tell us you were coming? we have not heard from you since my marriage.

Der.—The truth is, I was laid up with a touch of sunstroke, invalided for six months. I did not like to spoil your honeymoon with bad news. As soon as I regained my feet, they gave me six months leave, and I thought to take you by surprise.

Jos.—Dear old Jack ! I am glad to see you—how fat you have grown !

Der.—Yes—the sunstroke seems to have agreed with me.

Jos.—Mad as ever !

Der.—But you must present me to your husband. Where is Dove?

Jos —You arrive just in time to miss seeing him. He was here ten minutes ago. He has just started for Nottingham.

Der.—I am not sorry to have you all to myself for a few days.

Jos.—Oh, but you won't—he returns to-morrow.

Der.—Then let us make the most of to-day—you belong to yourself to-day—you are your own mistress !

Jos. (*laughing*).—And when my husband is here—I'm the master !

Der.—What a happy fellow ! What's his name? Scipio ?

Jos.—Cato.

Der.—True—I forgot. I knew it was something with an O. Well, we must spend the day together.

Jos.—We'll make a night of it !

Der.—So we will.

Jos.—Oh, what fun ! (*Kisses him.*)

Girl.—Oh !

(*Re-enter* Zulu L. H. *door.*)

Zulu.—I heard a familiar sound. Who's kissing so loud here) —it is against the rules of the company. (Josephine *crosses to* R.? Oh, it is my gunner !

Der. (C.) My lovely bombshell !

Zulu.—He is making the acquaintance of every girl he meets. Well, he did not get on as fast with me—she can't be much !

Jos. (R. *aside to* Der.)—Do you know this woman?

ZULU.—Woman! No more a woman than you are, ma'am—and much more of a lady. Good day, sir. (*Aside.*) Just like these common soldiers! (*Exit C.*)

Jos.—Oh, let us get away from this place as soon as possible.

DER.—Never mind her. Let us not mind anybody but our two happy selves. Recollect I have been four years away. Let us get a cab, and enjoy the rest of the day like two schoolboys. First, we'll dine at Richmond.

Jos.—I must go home, then, and change my dress.

DER.—I allow you fifteen minutes for the toilette.

Jos.—I'll make as much haste as if you were my lover.

DER.—Of course, you wouldn't hurry for a husband. After Richmond, we'll go to the Alhambra.

Jos.—Oh, Jack, is that proper?

DER.—Proper! It is the swell thing to do. There's a ballet, and I can smoke in the back of the box.

Jos.—I shall lose my reputation.

DER.—Leave it there—plenty of people in that place want one. Then, after the Alhambra, we'll go to Cremorne.

Jos.—Out of the frying pan into the fire. Jack, I dare not do it.

DER.—We can engage a private room overlooking the gardens —have a quiet little supper, and enjoy the fun.

Jos.—Enjoy the fun! What a heartless creature I should be to enjoy any fun while poor Cato is shaking and jolting along all night in that horrid railway carriage, on his road to Nottingham!

DER.—Do you think *he* would hesitate to embrace such an occasion as this because *you* could not share it?

Jos.—My dear Jack, you don't know him. I am his only occasion. He would embrace nothing whatever but me!

DER.—What a monotonous kind of a person he must be! Well, Josey, I'll be responsible for all the fun you will enjoy and I stick to my programme. Here is the ladies waiting-room; you must stay in here while I call up a cab.

Jos.—Don't be long. (*Exit into* R. H. *room.*)

Re-enter BUSTER, C. L. ; *he is nearly knocked down by* DERRINGER.

DER.—Can't you see where you are blundering to?

BUSTER.—Sir. I was just about to address the same question to you!

DER (*under his breath*)—Stupid old tailor! (*Exit.*)

29

BUSTER (*calling after him.*)—Why tailor! I don't perceive any-thing either ridiculous or degrading in the imputation—you may see it in that light—I don't! (*Comes down* L.) If he had waited I could have called him a volunteer, or a marine! These good ideas always occur to a fellow after he has lost the opportunity of expressing them. I have slipped through the matrimonial noose. When I got Mrs. Buster into the cab outside the station, I had a happy thought. "Arabella," I said, "we are close to the Agri-cultural Hall, where the Horse Show is in full force—the Royal Family will be there." (I baited the trap with that succulent lie.) "Shall we go?" She was delighted, and we drove to the Exhibi-tion. Two reserved seats in the gallery cost me half a sovereign. I had four pounds remaining of Cato's capital, so I did not mind the expense. When Arabella was safely squeezed in, after wading past forty people eighty knees, I jammed her in a remote stall, and waited beside her for an opportunity of giving her the slip—it soon came. She admired a pair of ponies—miserable rats, but they had long tails, and that captivated her. "Bella," I said, " you have taken a fancy to these pair of ponies? They shall be yours!" "Buster," she cried, "you don't mean it!" "Mean it," said I, you shall see, and I waded out. (*Looks at his watch.*) Let me see, it will take me to examine these ponies and get a medical certificate that they are both unsound in every limb, will take me three-quarters of an hour!

Re-enter CATO. *He is dressed in a long linen duster, and has a soft broad-brimmed hat.*

CATO —I have returned.

BUSTER.—Cato, where did you pick up that envelope?

CATO.—At the station at Hornsey. They sell them at the book-stall! Where's my wife?

BUSTER.—Safely at home!

CATO.—What a relief. I can breathe freely! now I am getting accustomed to the excitement, the sense of danger being past, I rather like the feeling!

BUSTER.—Don't you feel like a bird?

CATO.—Yes, but while my wife was in sight, the bird felt he was within shot, and the sensation is very unpleasant!

BUSTER.—Now you have an entire evening to enjoy yourself in our old bachelor fashion!

CATO —Yes. What shall we do to begin with?

BUSTER —Well, I must return to Arabella, (*looks at his watch,*) time's up. (Those ponies wont carry me any longer.) I left her at the Horse Show!

30

CATO.—You are not going to desert me?

BUSTER.—My dear fellow, I can't leave my wife in the middle of a horse show, I must take her home!

CATO —Of course; but after you have left her at home, where shall we meet—when—how?

BUSTER——She insists on my dining at home, and then taking her to the opera!

CATO.—But what am I to do all that time?

BUSTER.—Go to the Club!

CATO.—I can't; half the fellows know my wife, and I couldn't take them—the whole club—into our confidence!

BUSTER.—Go to Cremorne, dine there, and wait till I come.

CATO —Cremorne by daylight, before the lamps are lighted, with nobody but waiters and the checktakers on the premises! Can't you think of something that will occupy my time till nine o'clock?

BUSTER.—What do you say to a game of billiards?

CATO.—Splendid. I'll give you ten points in fifty, and play you for a sovereign!

BUSTER.—Don't I tell you I can't leave my wife?

CATO.—I'll give you fifteen points and make it a five pound note.

BUSTER.—Impossible!

CATO —But my dear fellow, consider my melancholy situation. I dare not show myself anywhere in town!

BUS.—Then take a cab and go for a drive in the country. My dear CATO, I proposed a night at Cremorne, but I did not undertake to find you employment for all the hours of the day. Stop! I know a quiet little public house, the Swan, at Chiswick, quite retired—not a soul there. They know me—take my card. (*Hands him a card*). 'I here you are! Have a tea dinner and a game of skittles with the landlord; he is a splendid fellow—will do anything for us. I defended him at the Old Bailey, case of burglary—got him off. He will treat you well—Bye-bye! Supper is ordered at 11; don't wait for me. I'll come, if I can! (*Exit C. D.*)

CATO.—This is not what I expected when I entertained the proposal to make a night of it! when I entertained a vague idea of reckless dissipation! the picture of a tea dinner in a retired public house did not present itself to my fevered imagination; a

burglar, however splendid, was not the lovely companion, and skittles was not the occupation I dreamed of. Oh, dear, I begin already to repent. I feel depressed in spirit. I would not dare to confess it to Buster, but I want to go home to Josey! Can't I make some excuse? I can say I was taken suddenly ill on the train! Yes, that would do! No—I forget! It wont do; for after we had retired to rest that infernal telegram will arrive from Nottingham. I can't explain being in a telegraph office at Nottingham and being in bed in London at the same time. That alibi would convict me.

(*Re-enter* BUSTER *hastily C. door*).

BUS. (L.)—Arabella is coming up the street; she has not seen me. I must slip around this way by the station and regain the horse show before she returns to the hall. (*Exit into railway station* L).

CATO (*runs up and looks off* R.)—Mrs. Buster, coming! What shall I do?

(*Enter* PODD C. *door*—*He looks up* L.)

PODD.—I just escaped the rain.

CATO.—Podd, my clerk, he must not recognize me! (*Turns to R. H. and pulls up his collar as he advances to R. C.*)

(PODD *going across to L. H. door.*)

POR.—The train for Kentish Town, Hempstead, Highgate?

PODD.—All right! I am going to Kentish Town. I'm just in time.

CATO (*at R. H. door.*) Where can I hide for one moment? (*He opens R. H. door—looks in suddenly—closes it.*) Oh, Lord, my wife! She's in there!

(PODD *at L. H. door, searches for his ticket to show the porter. A four wheel cab drives up to door in F. Enter* DERRINGER—*gets out of it.*)

DER. (*down* L.)—I thought I should never find a cab; this fellow is the only one on the stand. How it rains!

(*He crosses to* R H. *door and* CATO *runs up to C. door.*)

CATO.—Oh, dear! here comes Mrs. Buster. Podd blocks that door, and my wife is in there. I am surrounded on all sides. Oh! (*He opens the door of the cab and jumps in; closing it after him, he pulls down the blind.*)

(*Enter* JOSEY R. *Exit* PODD L.)

JOS.—What a time you have been! Have you found a cab?

32

DER.—All right—here it is !

(*Enter* MRS. BUSTER C. *door.*)

JOS.—Arabella, why where is the Serjeant ?

ARAB.—The monster, he left me in the horse show an hour ago ; it is all over. They turned me out. I am looking for him.

DER.—Now, jump in. (*Tries to open the door.*) It sticks very fast. (*He opens the door of the cab ; it is pulled to from the inside.*) Hallo ! what's that ? There is somebody inside.

CATO (*inside.*)—This cab is engaged.

DER. That's cool ; he says the cab is engaged ; of course it is. I engaged it, sir ; this cab is mine.

CATO. Drive on, coachman !

DER —Stop—not until I have your name.

CABMAN.—Now, then, aint you done ?

CATO (*putting out his arm offers a card.*) — There, sir. is my card ; take it.

DER. (*taking the card and advances.*)—I will hold you answerable wherever you are.

CATO (*putting his head out at front window.*)—Cabby, Putney Common ; a Sovereign if you gallop all the way.

CABMAN.— All right, sir. Hay ! (*He whips his horse. The cab disappears.*)

DER. (*reading card.*)—Mr. Sergeant Buster. Pump Court.

ARAB.—My husband ! (DERRINGER *rushes up and shakes his fist after the cab.*)

(*Bell rings.*)

POR. (*at door* L. H.)—Passengers for Bedford, Leicester, Derby, Manchester.

THE ACT DROP FALLS.

33

ACT III.

SCENE.—*Two rooms in a hotel, with the intermediate corridor. Doors in the partitions. Staircase and door at back. Supper tables laid.* SWALLBACH, *a German head waiter, seated in* R. H. *room.* JOSEPH, *a waiter, is holding a back of a fire shovel to his eye.*

SWALL. Ah! ce—ahee—Gott in himmel! I zall be plind my life.

JOSEPH. How did you do it?

SWALL. Ach! you vool. It vas not me It vas der gork der von champain bodel. (VICTOR *hurries in by corridor to* R. H. *room. He carries a bandage and a tomato.*) I vas open it. I gut der string, ven bom—it dos dam gork—he zhot me in de eye !

VIC. Here is the best thing in the world for a black eye.

SWALL. Vas ist das ? Ein domato !

VIC. Tomato ! the finest plaster !

JOSEPH. It aint to compare with a bit of raw beefsteak ! That's the reg'lar cure !

VIC Beefsteak ! You English imagine to yourselves the beefsteak is cure for everything.

SWALL. Sacrement, vile you vight vour beefsteak and domatoes, mine eye is glozing up. (*They bind the bandage over his eye, placing the tomato under it.*) Ach ! das vos goot, zo it is.

(*Bell rings.*)

VIC. There's the office bell !

SWALL Quick, it is bardy for supper. Make ready. (*He rises. Exit* VICTOR.)

(CATO *enters the corridor His hat is smashed His coat is covered with dirt and he wears a false nose.*)

CATO. This is what Buster calls making a night of it ! Buster drew out the programme. Buster composed the entertainment, I consented to play a part in the piece ; but if the incidents in store for the next three hours resemble what I have gone through already, I shall not live to see the morning. Waiter !

34

(Enter JOSEPH. SWALLBACH *and* VICTOR *light the lamps in* R. H. *rooms and exeunt.)*

JOSEPH. Sir, what can I get for you?

CATO. A clothes brush. *(Bell. Enter* VICTOR.)

JOSEPH. Coming, sir. Victor, the gentleman wants a brush.

CATO. Stop—there's a cab at the door. Ask the fellow what's his fare.

JOSEPH. How shall I know which cab it is, sir?

CATO. You can't mistake it. Look at me; the vehicle is in a similar condition; so is the horse. You will find the cabman inside, very drunk!

JOSEPH. All right, sir. *(Exit.)*

CATO. Now, I can release myself. *(Takes off his nose.)* Oh, what a relief that is! After achieving that hairbreadth escape from detection by my wife, we drove at a most illegal speed to Turnham Green; pulled up once in Knightsbridge to buy this nose. When I got to Chiswick I found I had forgotten the address of Buster's friend, the cheerful burglar. It was only half-past six o'clock and raining in torrents. The cabman said his horse was done up and as he had to go home to change his animal, I pulled out my purse—you cannot picture my despair when I found I had given all my money—five pounds—to Buster! I was obliged to stick to that cab. I have passed the evening in that cab. The fellow drove me home—to a stable-yard in the Old Kent Road. There he took out the horse and left me in the cab for two hours, at half a crown an hour. It was raining in torrents for two hours. He came back—drunk! Oh, so drunk that even the horse seemed to look on in doubt as to the propriety of trusting him with the reins I had no alternative. I put him inside, mounted the box and drove the vehicle myself. It was raining in torrents. All went fairly—I may say swimmingly—till I tried to pass a dust cart in Millbank; caught the hind-wheel, and over we went. I landed amongst the ash-barrels. A friendly policeman soon put us right again. The cabman inside did the swearing, and I drove here!

(Re-enter JOSEPH.)

JOSEPH. The man says it is two sovereigns, sir, you promised to give him.

CATO. One The rogue sees double.

JOSEPH. Well, sir, he says if you won't pay it he wants your number.

35

Cato. My number?

Joseph. You had best take his, sir, and give him your card.

Cato (*Aside.* Oh, the deuce! that would never do! (*Aloud.*) Pay the fellow what he asks, and put it on the bill.

Joseph. What name, sir? Who shall we charge to?

Cato. My name; oh, charge it to Buster I am going to sup here with Serjeant Buster's party.

Cato (*takes off his duster and hat—gives them to* Joseph.)

Joseph. The Serjeant is well known to us here, sir. Quite right, sir! (*Exit.*)

(*Enter* Victor *with a brush.*)

Vic. Here is a brush, sir—is that all for the present?

(Victor *brushing him.*)

Cato. You don't think a man who has eaten nothing since half-past eight this morning can stay his stomach with a clothes-brush? I want a room—the best, warmest, cosiest, you have and supper for four.

Vic. Here is the very thing, sir. We kept this for Mr. Buster's party. (*Showing* Cato *into* L. H R)

Cato (*looking around.*) Very snug—uncommonly snug—but what door is that?

Vic. (*opening door in flat.*) It slides back, sir; so as to throw the two rooms into one when we have a large party.

Cato. Ah! very convenient, but on this occasion if you have another party in there, they can overhear all that passes in this room. Have you not something more private?

Vic Step this way, sir; here is the very room you require—(*Enters* R. H. *room*)—quite retired; tiled in, sir, with a window overlooking the gardens.

Cato. Excellent! Your name?

Vic. Victor!

Cato. Here's a crown for you! (*Feels in his pocket.*)

Vic. Thank you, sir!

Cato Put it in the bill—charge it to Buster! Now for the supper. I am as empty as a drum!

(*Enter* Swallbach.)

Vic. The Head Waiter will take your orders, sir!

Cato. I feel as if I could eat an elephant roast and drink the

36

Rhine   Has the supper been ordered ?

Swal. Not a yed, sir; de Zergent he lete it do me.

Cato (*Aside.*) Who is this foreign Cyclops ?

Swall. Ed a vayter, sir, to zerve you !

Cato. From Servia ? So I should think from your appearance —got a Bashi Bazook in the eye?

Swall. Nein, a gork in de eye, sir, in Champayne.

Cato. Ah ! reminiscence of the French war. Well, now for supper. Supper for four. Let me see—oysters, anchovy toast, cold salmon, a spatchcock, a lobster salad take care the insect is fresh ; half a dozen woodcocks, broiled—nicely underdone — on toast ; dessert and Roman punch !

Swall. (*repeats to himself the list as he writes it down.*) Hysters, to set anchut; Solomon gold, mit a despatcher cock; zalad, mit lobster, afterwards a would-be cock, broil on toset, unterdone, mit Punch Romaine in de desert ! Now vor de wein !

Cato. Champagne—two bottles dry.

Swall: Doo bodles ! in der middle of four beeples—it is eight boddles !

Cato. Go it—eight bottles—they have got to last all night.

Swall. Und dis is vor your aggount—to your name !

Cato. No ; Buster. Change it to Sergeant Buster only serve it as soon as you can, and Victor——

Vic. Monsieur.

Cato. If any one calls for Mr. Alfred—I expect a lady—two ladies—you will show them in here ; don't admit any one else !

Vic. All right, sir. (*Exit.*)

Cato (*Aside.*) I think I am pretty safe at last—snugly tiled in, no one will recognize me here. (*Aloud.*) You understand that I am Herr Alvred !

Swall. Yaw, zir ; anything you vish—you can rely on us, Mr. Dove. (*Going.*)

Cato. What did he say ? What remark did that Polyphemus make !

Swall. If I had mein eye—mitout dis—dot it is you shall not vorget Smallbach, of de Cafe de la Mad'laine, Paris, vere you come so often to dine mit dot putiful lady !

Cato. (*Aside.*) My wife ! (*Aloud.*) You mistake me for ano- ther person. I'm often confounded with him—he's a—a Scotchman from—a—Derbyshire. I'm an American just arrived from—a—

the Centennial—why, certainly—don't you hear, I'm an American, I am !

SWALL. Zertainly—yaw—I gompre-end, I didn't see before. I make mistake.

CATO. Of course, how can you remember me with only one eye !

SWALL Dass a fax.

CATO. My name is Tyler—Dewitt Q. Tyler, of Tippecanoe, New Jersey—you will recollect ?

SWALL. Yaw, Mr. Dove. I vill not forget.

CATO Tyler !

SWALL. I understand, Mr. Dove ; don't be avraid I vorget. (*Exit.*)

CATO. That could not happen to anyone but me ! now I must buy the discretion of that one-eyed monster at any price. I must charge him to Buster. (*Looks at his wa'ch.*) Five minutes to 11, and not a soul arrived to relieve my solitary misery. Six hours since I parted from my wife—it seems like six months—and this is making a night of it. May I never make another ! Oh, Josephine ! if you knew how I am being served out ! You can't hear me swear, but I do, never again to go and *try the taste of forbidden fruit !*

Enter BUSTER, C.

BUSTER Waiter, which is Mr. Alfred's room ?

JOSEPH. (*Meeting him.*) This way, sir.

CATO. BUSTER—at last !

BUSTER. If you knew what I have gone through to get here—

CATO. Take it, put it under a microscope, magnify it 40,000 times, and you will see the horrible secrets of my life during the last six hours ! but the clouds have cleared away. "The night has passed, and joy cometh with the morrow." Now we will enjoy ourselves, eh ?

BUSTER. I wish I could, but it is impossible.

CATO. What ?

BUSTER. I can't stop. I have left my wife at the Opera ; took a Hansom cab, and came down here to tell you how unfortunate it has turned out.

CATO. Unfortunate !

BUSTER. I am in a worse fix than you are. I'm obliged to give up this party.

CATO. What—give me up ?

38

BUSTER. I must run back to my wife, who—(*looking at his watch*)—I left at the Opera. I had the greatest difficulty in persuading her she was in fault this afternoon, when I left her at the Horse Show. I can't play the same card twice in one hand.

CATO. And you are going to leave me with these two ladies that you have invited?

BUSTER. Don't be alarmed. I have telegraphed Closerie not to come—I have put her off.

CATO. Put her off?

BUSTER. Certainly, and I have no doubt she has told Zulu—so neither of them will come.

CATO. But what am I to do?

BUSLER. Go home !

CATO. Go home !—I can't. You forget I am at Nottingham ! how can I explain my return ?

BUSTER Say the locomotive broke down on the road.

CATO. How can I? at ten o'clock, according to your calculation, she received my telegram to say I had arrived there safely.

BUSTER. What the devil did you telegraph for? If you will spoil your wife by acceding to her caprices, you must accept the consequences.

CATO. I hope you are not going to leave me in for it !

BUSTER. In for it ! I like that. I found you closeted with a lovely girl this afternoon—you agreed with me to have a jovial night of it. Here you are. I wish you joy, old man. I must be off. (*Exit.*) I have barely time to reach the Opera. (*Disappears off at* C.)

CATO. But stop. Where am I to sleep? I can't go home ; I can't prolong supper until 9 in the morning—that is the earliest hour I can decently present myself in Bolton Row. I shall be turned out of this place at 2 in the morning, then I must ramble about in the rain. It is raining in torrents still. I shall go and walk in front of my own house, look up at the windows (*Re-enter* JOSEPH *with glasses.*) not daring to enter ; regarded with suspicion by the policeman. Oh, waiter ! I ordered supper for four.

JOS. It is ready, sir !

CATO. Be good enough to say I only want it for one.

JOS. Impossible, sir. It is too late now. It is cooked and coming up. (*Exit.*)

CATO. But I can't eat all that ; it will look absurd. (*Enter*

39

VICTOR *and* SMALLBACH *with dishes.*) It is ridiculous. I can't sit down before all that, alone. I'll take a look into the coffee room, and if I see a congenial fellow there, I'll invite him to share my supper. (*Re enter* JOSEPH, *preceeding* DERRINGER.)

Jos. This way, sir.

DER I want a quiet room for a lady and myself. (JOSEPH *enters* L. H *Room as* DERRINGER *follows him.* CATO *enters corridor* C.)

CATO. I'll invite the first I —— By Jove, here's the very thing ! There's a military jovial cut about him I like.

DER. This will do. I will go down and bring the lady. (*Re-enters corridor.*)

CATO. Sir, I beg your pardon.

DER Did you speak to me ?

CATO. Yes, sir I did myself that honor. I am a stranger here, you seem to be another.

DER. I arrived in London this evening.

CATO. In the army ?

DER. Yes, sir.

CATO. So am I—that is, I am in the 21st Middlesex, Lawyers Corps. Further ceremony is useless. Will you do me the pleasure of supping with me ?

DER. You are very kind. Another time I should be very happy to improve your acquaintance, but I have a lady waiting for me in a cab at the door, so you must excuse me.

CATO. You are going to sup with a lady. Happy fellow, I envy you. I was in a similar condition——

DER. I hope you will allow me——

CATO. I understand——

DER. (*To* JOSEPH.) Lay supper for two——

CATO. Sir, your lady does not happen to have a female friend with her ? If so, it would just suit me, for I have supper ready for four, and we could——

DER. (*Stiffly.*) No, sir, the lady is not the kind of person you mistake her for. Good evening ! (*Exit.*)

CATO I have no luck. (*Exit* JOSEPH.)

SWALL. De table is zerved !

CATO. (*Entering his room*) For four (SMALLBACH *goes up corridor*) My appetite is gone ! (*Sits.*) I shall not forget this party of pleasure in a hurry. Supper for four !

40

VICTOR. Do you want anything else?

CATO. (*Rising furiously.*) Yes. I want to break your head! (VICTOR *runs out.*) The sight of those 3 empty chairs is a hollow mockery. (*Takes off the covers.*) Where on earth shall I put all that. Oh, I wish my wife was here! (*Enter* SMALLBACH *with four bottles of Champagne followed by* JOSEPH *with four bottles.*) What is that?

SWALL. The champagne, sir, eight boddles——

CATO. You don't imagine I am going to drink eight bottles of wine?

SWALL. Eight boddles vas order. Eight boddles vos put on the ice. And ven it is ice it must be trunk. It is already in de bill! (*Exit* JOSEPH.)

CATO. All right, charge it to Buster!

SWALL. Vera goot, Mr. Dove——

CATO. Tyler!

SWALL. I sall not vorgot. I am tiscreet, Mr. Dove! (*Exit.*)

CATO. The Dutch idiot! He made me swallow an oyster the wrong way!

Enter DERRINGER *and* JOSEPHINE *by corridor into* L. H. *room.*

DER. This way. (*They enter* L. H. *Room.*)

JOS. Oh, this is charming! What a delightful day we have spent! There was only one drawback to my complete satisfaction, and that was the absence of my poor Cato. I wonder what he is doing now?

DER. Sound asleep, I dare say; what a spooney little darling you are? You made me drive all the way round by your house in Bolton Row to find that telegram.

JOS. (*Reads*) 62 Bolton Row, London. Dear old Catydid—I do spoil him!

CATO. Oh, Lord! I wonder what my wife is doing now! Snug in bed, no doubt, dreaming of me. I wish she were here—or I was there!

(*Enter* VICTOR *with the dishes to* L. H *room.*)

VIC. There are the oysters to begin with—what will you please order to follow?

DER. Josephine, you must select the supper.

JOS. Must I? Let me see.

(JOSEPHINE *writes with pencil on paper which* VICTOR *hands to her.*)

JOS. I'll ruin you with a delicious bill of fare.

41

C<small>ATO</small>. This bird is done to a cinder. I'll try the lobster—I used to be fond of lobster. (*Eats*) What's this—white India rubber, flavored with phosphorus? Oh, this won't do! (*Rings the bell.*)

V<small>IC</small>. (*Shouting from other room.*) Coming, sir.

J<small>OS</small>. There I think that will be exquisite!

D<small>ER</small>. Let the champagne be dry and not too cold.

V<small>IC</small>. (*Taking the list.*) Very good, sir.

C<small>ATO</small>. Will they never answer the bell—(*rings furiously*) or must I tear the bell out by the roots?

(V<small>ICTOR</small> *crossing into* R. H. *room.*)

V<small>IC</small>. Coming, sir. (*As he crosses he cries to* S<small>WALBACH</small>) Monopole dry for No. 9.

C<small>ATO</small>. Oh, you are here at last!

V<small>IC</small>. Beg pardon, sir, I was serving the party in the next room.

C<small>ATO</small>. Take that insect away—disinfect it, and—what do you call that bird?

V<small>IC</small>. Woodcock, sir.

C<small>ATO</small>. Yes, it is the woodenest I ever sat down to—take it away!

V<small>IC</small>. What would you like instead, sir?

C<small>ATO</small>. How do I know? I can't choose—I can't think! What has that party ordered in the next room?

V<small>IC</small>. Here is their bill of fare, sir.

C<small>ATO</small>. Let me see what they are going to indulge in.

(S<small>WALB</small>.<small>CH</small> *entering* L. H. R. *with wine.*)

S<small>WAL</small>. Dry Monopole. (*Places bottle on table.*) Any oder ting, sir?

D<small>ER</small>. Yes—brandy and soda.

S<small>WALL</small>. Vera goot, sir. (*Exit.*)

C<small>ATO</small> (*Reading*). Chicken salad—why it can't be! This is the writing of my wife!

V<small>IC</small>. What, sir?

C<small>ATO</small>. Nothing—I am deceived. Truffled partridge, macaroni Italienne. 'hose I's are Josephine's—I'd swear to her I's a mile off! My wife here! in such a place as this—at this time of night, when I am at Nottingham! Oh, dear! Waiter!

V<small>IC</small>. Sir! .

C<small>ATO</small>. What sort of persons are in the adjoining room?

42

Vɪᴄ Oh, sir—I—really—you must not ask me.

Cᴀᴛᴏ. Speak! I'll—here's a five pound note.

Vɪᴄ. Well, sir ?

Cᴀᴛᴏ. Put it on the bill—charge it to Buster. But, speak, who is there ?

Vɪᴄ. A lady, sir.

Cᴀᴛᴏ. Good figure—brown hair—regular features?

Vɪᴄ. Yes, sir, that's it.

Cᴀᴛᴏ. Dressed in blue ?

Vɪᴄ. Blue and grey.

Cᴀᴛᴏ. She is alone, or with another lady ?

Vɪᴄ. The other lady aint arrived yet, sir ; she is with an officer. I think the gentleman is ——

Cᴀᴛᴏ. An elderly man, aint he ?

Vɪᴄ. About twenty-six. You don't look well, sir !

Cᴀᴛᴏ. It is the lobster !

Vɪᴄ. Is that all you require, sir ?

Cᴀᴛᴏ. All I require? Get out—go! (Vɪᴄᴛᴏʀ *exits*.) All I require. It is very much more than I require I cannot believe it to be possible, my wife—my Josephine—here—there—with a soldier. I'll not believe it. (*Entering the corridor.*) No one here What terrible truth am I about to discover through this keyhole ? (*Looks through the keyhole* L H. *room.*) There they are ; she is looking down; he is stooping over her. It is the young fellow I met here just now ; his arm is 'round her—now she looks up. Ah ! 'tis, 'tis she—my wife—Josey. I am losing my senses !

Dᴇʀ You little fool, what is that paper ?

Cᴀᴛᴏ. Hush ! they speak, he called her "a little fool."

Jos. It is the billet deux I received from Cato !

Cᴀᴛᴏ. She is never going to read him my love letters—to feed him with my spoon !

Jos. Listen, (*she reads the telegram*) " Your darling one arrived here very sad—

Cᴀᴛᴏ. It is my telegram from Nottingham.

Jos. (*reading*) Far from his Josey." What a wretched night he will pass --

Cᴀᴛᴏ. The spirit of prophecy was on me when I wrote that.

Jos. (*reads*) But to-morrow, your faithful Bogamps will embrace you, his beloved.

Dᴇʀ. Bogamps?

43

Jos. That's a foolish pet name I gave him.

Cato. How well I remember the moment!

Der. Well, old girl, I dare say he would not be sorry to be in my place.

Cato. In his place. They are turning me into ridicule; he calls her "old girl." What shall I do? (*Enter* Swalbach *with brandy and soda*). Who is that? Where are you going with that wine?

Swall. To the bardy in No. 9.

Cato. Stop - yes—that's a splendid idea. I—I'll do it—let me look at you!

Swall. Excoos me!

Cato. Stop, I tell you. Will you earn ten pounds, fifteen, twenty?

Swall. Zwanzig?

Cato. Lend me your apron—your bandage, all right!

Swall. Vat vor?

Cato. Twenty pounds; hold that. (*Pulls off his bandage and gives him to hold while he puts on the apron, then the bandage, and finally takes the Nose from his pocket and puts it on*) Now give me your bottles of wine?

Swall. But I do not comprehend.

Cato. Twenty pounds; put it in the bill; charge it to Buster—all right!

Swall. Ah! it is a joke, I zee—a joke mit dose beeples.

Der. Are those fellows never going to bring the wine? (*He rings the bell violently.*)

Swall. Gomming!

Cato. Clear out. (*Threatens* Swalbach, *who runs out.*)

Der. Oh, here it is at last!

Enter Cato *to* L. H. *room.*)

Cato, Gomming—yaw, mynheer—der wein— vat it is!

(Victor *and* Joseph *bring dishes into* L. H *room, lay them on table and exeunt.*)

Der. Supper at last. Now, Josey, sit down!

Cato (*flourishing the bottle behind* Derringer's *back*) I'll Josey him!

Jos. What a singular looking waiter!

Der. He has only one eye, but that's a blazer!

(Cato *opens bottle of wine and pours out three tumblers; hands them on salver.*)

44

CATO (*aside*) I would like to break his head with the bottle !

Jos. (*taking a glass*) I was dying with thirst.

DER. (*taking a glass*) The fellow has poured out a third glass of wine. Don't you see there are only two of us, idiot?

C..TO. Yaw—ein—zwei—drei—I but it avay. (*Retires and drinks it.*)

DER. What are you doing? Are you out of your senses or drunk?

CATO. You object to it, so I put it avay.

DER. Leave the room—we wish to be alone (DERRINGER *speaks to* JOSEPHINE.)

CATO. (*Aside.*) They want to be alone The shameless woman. (*Sits down.*) She hears him avow his desire to be alone with her, and she does not –

DER. (*Turns and sees him sitting down.*) Will you get out?

CATO. (*Rises.*) (*Aside.*) She laughs. (*Aloud.*) I go. (*Gains the door.*) Oh, if I wasn't at Nottingham. (*Turns.*) If you sall vant any tings, you ring, and I am here.

DER. Go to the devil !

CATO Ring always, as ofden as you blease. (DERRINGER *offers to throw the bottle at him.* CATO *shuts the door—he listens.*)

Jos. I do believe the poor fellow is crazy—there is something the matter with his head.

CATO. That's where it is !

DER. My darling Josey, you don't drink.

CATO. His darling !

Jos. Yes, I do Jack.

CATO. He darlings her, and she Jacks him ! (*Looking through the key-hole.*) I won't lose a word, nor a look—nor a gesture. Oh, dear ! I can't see. Hush ! they are not speaking—that's a bad sign What can they have to whisper about? It is not allowed in a respectable house. Hush ! dead silence !

DER. (*After drinking again.*) Oh, that's lovely ! (CATO *bursts in on them*)

CATO. Gomming ! (JOSEPHINE *screams.*)

DER. Are you mad ?

CATO. Don't you vant zometing?

DER. What the mischief brings you here?

CATO. (*As he retires.*) It was nothing—false alarm. (*Meets* VICTOR, *who enters with salad, he takes it.*) Salade !

DER. Put it down there ; take these things away.

Jos. (*Aside*) How the creature eyes me.

45

DER. (*Aside to her.*) Don't be afraid. (CATO *puts the salad on table—removes the dishes.*) This salad is not mixed—where's the oil and vinegar?

CATO. Gomming.

DER. Waiter—champagne!

CATO. Gomming. (*Brings the oil and champagne, aside, looking at* J. SEPHINE.) I wish it was prussic acid and strychnine. (*He pours the oil in her glass and the champagne in the salad.*)

JOS. Oh, what is he doing he's helping me to oil.

DER. And pouring champagne in the salad. Will you get out and send us another waiter?

CATO. (*Aside, going out.*) He orders me out. (*Bitterly*) Ah! This is making a night of it! (*He listens.*)

DER. I'll stop further impertinent intrusion. (*He locks the door.*)

CATO. He has locked the door.

DER. There now, we are rid of that idiot. I hope you have enjoyed your evening.

JOS. It has been delightful.

CATO. They have spent all the evening together.

JOS. It reminds me of the days we spent together five years ago, when we used to steal out together unknown to my uncle, and you took me to see the fireworks at the Crystal Palace.

CATO. I am seeing fireworks now.

DER. What fun we used to have.

CATO. Oh it has been going on for five years.

JOS. My dear Jack you were the only being in the world I had to love ; and if you knew how I cried my eyes out when you joined your regiment.

DER. Dear old girl! (*He kisses her hand.*)

CATO. He kissed her—I heard it!

JOS. But now, I shall see you every day.

DER. Certainly.

JOS. I shall introduce you to my husband.

CATO. Of course!

JOS. You will dine with us every day?

CATO. I must take him in to board.

JOS. You and Cato will get on splendidly. Why can't you come and stop with us altogether? I'm sure Cato wouldn't mind it!

CATO. Oh! Oh! Not mind it!

46

Jos. There is some one at that door. I heard a noise!

Cato. What are they about? (*Looks through keyhole.*)

Derr. Surely, that Dutch scoundrel cannot be listening. If he is, I will teach him to attend to his own business. (*He opens the door suddenly.* Cato *tumbles in.* Derr *seizes him.*) What were you doing there?

Jos. Oh, Jack, don't, pray don't.

Cato. Let me go!

Derr. Not until I throw you out of the window!

(*In the struggle* Cato's *bandage and his nose falls off.*)

Cato. Oh, my nose!

Jos. My husband—it can't be you it is!

Derr. Your husband?

Jos. Why, Cato, what brings you here?

Cato. No, madam, that is not the question. I prefer to ask what brings you here? Sir, I am the unfortunate husband of that lady, who has not been the dupe she has imagined. This afternoon I pretended to leave for Nottingham

Jos. Pretended!

Cato. It was a trap, madam, to detect you as I have done. I have followed you in disguise all day. I have been a witness to your conduct with this gentleman, whom you call your darling Jack. Don't deny it; it is useless.

Jos. I don't deny it. This is my brother, Jack Derringer

Cato. Your brother! No! no!

Jos. Who returned from India this evening.

Derr. And who certainly did not anticipate the pleasure of meeting you in this manner.

Cato. Oh, my angel! Oh, forgive me — if you knew — I thought—your hand Porringer; forgive me.

Derr. Derringer!

Cato. I beg your pardon. I am so confused—I mean so relieved.

Jos. And you really suspected me capable of acting such a part? Oh! Oh!

Cato. No! no! I didn't that is, I was a jealous fool!

Derr. (*Lighting a cigar.*) It is past now. Let us forget and forgive.

Cato. I do—I forgive.

Jos. Oh, Jack don't smoke here, please; it always makes me ill.

47

DERR. All right, Josey; I'll take a turn in the garden and leave you together.

CATO. Let him smoke. You shall smoke all over my house. I am so grateful to him for being your brother. He shall do whatever he likes!

DERR. That's hearty. I'll take up my quarters with you. Sling me a berth in any corner – brother Jack is not particular.

(Exit by corridor.)

CATO. Josey, Josey, throw your arms around me—take me home! Oh, if you only knew how I have loved you all this blessed—I would say infernal evening. Oh, never let us part again!

JOS. You dearest of foolish fellows! Do you think I regret your jealousy? Why, I am delighted you were miserable, for it shows the depth of your love for me. What! you have been suspecting me? That's delicious! And spying after me? Oh, Cato, you darling. there are so few husbands now-a-days, that love their wives well enough to be jealous of them!

CATO. Love you? Josey, I adore you! I never look at any other woman ! (CATO *embraces* JOSEPHINE.)

(Enter ZULU *and* JOSEPH *into corridor.)*

ZULU. Which is Mr. Alfred's room? I am late.

JOSEPH. Mr. Alfred? (*Bell rings.*) Coming the room on your right. (*Exit.*)

(Zulu as he speaks has her back to audience.)

ZULU. On my right. Oh, this is it; No. 9. Here goes; of course Closerie has not come.

(Zulu knocks at L H. *door.)*

JOS. Some one is knocking. Oh, perhaps it is Jack, who has finished his smoke. Why does he knock?

CATO. He means it as a delicate attention. Dear old Jack!

(*He opens door, sees* ZULU *and shuts it.*) (*Aside.*) Oh, Lord, Zulu!

ZULU. (*Knocking.*) Don't shut the door, it's me!

JOS. Who is it?

(CATO keeping door shut and locking it.)

CATO. Nobody! It is an old gentleman who—who—has mistaken the room!

ZULU (*Knocking.*) Are you going to open the door? Come, I say, Alfred, none of your larks.

48

Jos. There, he is knocking again!

Cato No; it is next door, I assure you!

Zulu. Will you open the door? Oh, don't be a fool!

Jos. Do see what the man wants.

Cato. Never mind him—he will go away when he's tired. (*Aside*) Oh, dear, what shall I do?

Jos. I will send him about his business. (*Goes to door.*)

Cato. I am lost! Where can I retire? Oh, if I could subside into my boots! (*Sees the door in* F.) Ah, the next room!

(*Slides back door, disappears as* Josephine, *opens door* R. *and admits* Zulu.)

Jos. A lady!

Zulu I beg your pardon. Where is Alfred?

Jos. I beg yours, madam; there is no Alfred here.

Zulu. So I see. but he *was* here. We met this morning, and he invited me to sup with him this evening.

Jos. *My* husband invited *you* to sup here! It is false, ma'am, I won't believe it!

Zulu. Your husband! In what acceptation of the word, madam?

Jos. Oh, I can't stand this! (Cato *appears in corridor.*)

Zulu. Nor can I. Where is he? I'll teach him to play the fool with me. Oh, here's another room! (*Exit door in* F. *followed by* Josephine, *as* Cato *enters* R. H. *Room and locks door.*)

Cato. Just escaped that explosive female! but how shall I explain my disappearance to Josey? I am becoming enmeshed in a web of lies. Caught in my own pretences. I wish I had Buster here to help me! (*Enter* Buster *in corridor.*)

Buster. I left Arabella at home. I said I would go out in our square to smoke a cigar, and here I am!

Cato. I don't hear the raging of the wild animals!

Buster. (*Trying door* R. H. *Room.*) Locked on the inside! (*Knocks.*) Sympathy teaches us discretion.

Cato. There she is!

Buster. (*Whispering.*) Whist! 'Tis I!

Cato. Oh, yes. I'm going to let you in—in a hurry!

(*Re-enter* Josephine *into* L. H. *Room.*)

Jos. Where can Cato be? He was not there. He must have gone out by this door! (*As she opens door she meets* Buster.)

49

BUSTER. MRS. Dove ! here !

JOS. Oh, Sergeant, how glad I am to see you ! (BUSTER *enters* L. H. *Room*.) Where's my husband ?

BUSTER. He's at Nottingham !

JOS. No, he is here !

BUSTER. Here ? It can't be ; you are mistaken !

JOS. I tell you I saw him !

BUSTER. It must have been an optical—er—delusion.

(CATO *who has been listening inside his door*.)

CATO. I'll take a peep, and if I find the road is clear, I will run for it !

JOS. (*Sitting down and holding her head in helpless confusion*.) Am I going mad ?

(*Re-enter* DERRINGER *down corridor*.)

DER. Surely that lady talking to the waiter must be my little bombshell friend in the artillery !

CATO Porringer ! I am saved ! Come, come in here ! (*Drags* DERRINGER *into* R. H. *Room and closes door*.)

DER. What's the matter ?

JOS. I spoke to him, I tell you ; he followed me.

BUSTER. Where to—have you been to Nottingham ?

JOS. Oh, you are all in a plot to drive me out of my senses !

CATO. I am in a frightful mess. You can save me, if you will. Not for my sake, but for hers—for Josey's. Listen ! (CATO *speaks apart to* DERRINGER.)

(*Re-enter* ZULU *with* VICTOR.)

VICTOR. You mistook the room, Miss, this is **Mr. Alfred's** room.

ZULU (*Entering* R. H. *Room*.) Ah ! there you are !

DER. (*To* ZULU.) Keep quiet. It is all a mistake. (*To* CATO.) I understand it all. Leave it to me. I'll pull you through !

ZULU. I declare, it is my friend in the artillery.

(*Enter* ARABELLA, *in corridor with* JOSEPH. DERRINGER, ZULU *and* CATO *speak apart*.)

ARAB. So, you say Sergeant Buster has a supper party here, to-night ?

JOSEPH. Yes, ma'am ; one of the ladies is here—the other——

ARAB. One is enough, sir ! (*Exit* JOSEPH.)

BUS. My dear soul—don't take on so !

50

ARAB. That's his voice ! He's with her in here !

Jos. Don't leave me !

Bus. I must get back to my wife, or she will suspect something is wrong.

ARAB. (*Bursting into* L. H. *room.*) Villain ! I have detected you at last ! Josephine—Oh ! it was Mrs. Dove ! This is too much !

Jos What ! do you dare to insinuate, madam, that you entertain any doubts about me?

ARAB. None whatever, ma'am ! The place, the position in which I find you, leaves no room for any doubt whatever.

Jos. Oh this is too much ! (JOSEPHINE *rings the bell furiously.*)

DER. Rejoin your wife at once ; we will follow you.

CATO. Zulu—Porringer—I shall owe you my life ! (CATO *crosses from* R. H. *room to* L. H. *room.*)

ARAB. While your infatuated idiot of a husband is at Notting ham, you replace your fool with my knave. Cato !

' ATO. Go on, Mrs. Buster. Take it out of me. I am used to it this evening.

Jos. Cato, you will explain to that lady how I came here.

CATO. (*Dignified.*) My wife, madam, came here with her husband—with me !

Jos. She charged me with impropriety.

CATO. If she entertains such charges against any one here, charge them to Buster !

(*Enter* DERRINGER *with* ZULU.)

DER. I am sorry to confess I am to blame for all this. Allow me to explain. On my arrival this afternoon I met this lady, an old friend of mine and I invited her to sup here to-night. Miss— a— (*Aside.*) What's your name ?

ZULU. Zulu !

DERR. Miss Zulu, accepted the invitation, and in the excitement of meeting my sister, I totally forgot all about it. Miss Lulu came——

ZULU. Zulu !

DERR. Found her place occupied.

Jos. Ah. then you were the Alfred she wanted ?

DERR. Yes : she always called me Alfred as a—a—short for Jack. We are such old friends. I——

51

ARAB. Stop, stop, this is all very clear so far; but when I arrived here, the waiter downstairs told me that supper had been ordered for two ladies by Sergeant Buster.

CATO (*Aside.*) Now he's in for it—go it—charge it to Buster.

BUSTER. By *me*—ordered by *me!* Where is the waiter?

(*Enter* SWALLBACH.)

SWALL. Gomming, sir. Here is der bill!

ARAB. (*Taking it.*) Twenty-seven pounds six.

JOS. Oh, what can they have had to come to that?

BUSTER. No, no; I appeal. My lords and gentlemen of the —that is—I forgot. This is absurd! (*Aside.*) Oh! the luxury of being falsely accused! It is a new sensation!

DERR. Allow me to explain further. When I ordered supper for this lady and her friend the waiter asked me for my name, and I handed them my card, as I thought. By mistake, I gave them a card I received from a scoundrel of the name of Buster, who stole my cab this afternoon!

BUSTER Arabella, tell him that was not *me;* say it was some *other* scoundrel. Save your husband's honor!

ARAB. It could not have been you, for I found you waiting for me at the Horse Show. I will do you that justice!

BUSTER. Virtue is triumphant!!!

CATO. Who could it have been?

SWALL. Das ist vera good; but who is to pay the bill?

DERR. I'll settle it! (*to* ZULU.) I think the supper is ready in the other room. (*Exit* ZULU *into* R. H. *Room.*)

CATO. No we can't allow you to pay! (*He takes the bill from* SWALLBACH.) Can we Charley? We demur. Waiter, this is our affair. Buster, we must settle this.

(*Exit* SWALLBACH *into* R. H. *Room.*)

(BUSTER *and* CATO *follow* SWALLBACH *into corridor.* DERRINGER *takes the wine and pours out glasses full for the ladies.*)

DERR. Come, ladies, in the absence of your husbands, let us drink a toast!

CATO. (*Drawing* BUSTER *forward.*) My dear fellow! one word with you. You tempted me to make what you called a night of it!

BUSTER. You did not know how to make one!

CATO. Possibly! but I'll never attempt to make another! I have tried the taste of forbidden fruit. I don't like it! A fast

life looks charming to those who see it as spectators look at a play, but you have introduced me behind the scenes, and I prefer the illusion to the reality !

BUSTER. (*Mournfully.*) There is no illusion about Arabella.

DERR. Now, ladies, are you ready ?

CATO. (*Listening.*) Hush !

JOS. Here's to my darling, Cato—the best, truest, most devoted of husbands.

BUSTER. Do you hear ?

CATO. I do, and I blush !

ARAB. Here's to my dear old Charley, whom I confess I have wronged by my suspicions.

(*The ladies drink.*)

CATO. And you said there was no illusion about her ! Oh, Charley, Charley ! if you found your wife out in such infidelity as you indulge in daily. Ah ! what would you say ?

BUSTER, (*Wiping away a tear.*) I'd say—charge it to Buster ! !

They embrace—as the ladies drink the toast the

CURTAIN FALLS.

www.ingramcontent.com/pod-product-compliance
Lightning Source LLC
Chambersburg PA
CBHW020808020726
47495CB00008B/2639